Sofo Rox

By
Sophie Bicker and Kenny Bicker

AuthorHouse™ UK
1663 Liberty Drive
Bloomington, IN 47403 USA
www.authorhouse.co.uk
UK TFN: 0800 0148641 (Toll Free inside the UK)
UK Local: 02036 956322 (+44 20 3695 6322 from outside the UK)

Because of the dynamic nature of the Internet, any web addresses or links contained in this book may have changed since publication and may no longer be valid. The views expressed in this work are solely those of the author and do not necessarily reflect the views of the publisher, and the publisher hereby disclaims any responsibility for them.

Any people depicted in stock imagery provided by Getty Images are models, and such images are being used for illustrative purposes only.
Certain stock imagery © Getty Images.

This book is printed on acid-free paper.

ISBN: 978-1-6655-8919-2 (sc)
ISBN: 978-1-6655-8918-5 (e)

Print information available on the last page.

Published by AuthorHouse 05/12/2021

authorHOUSE

Table of Contents

Sofo and the Shadow-Witch 49

Characters

Sofo -the scientist-explorer
Floof - Sofo's dog/ assistant
Rhyco- the cloud fixer
Kroxy Jnr -the Goth Janny
MizJojo -Lady Rox
Kroxalot -The Explorer
Dabidee - Unicorn rider
Cruella – Unicorn rider
Bur - Cloud rider
Twiggs - Cloud rider
Pandoo- The chop shop owner
Jimbob - The glitter farmer
Pee-Lee – Jimbob's pal
Penny - The Cheerleader
Handsome Dave - Commando from Japan
Applejack - Unicorn
Jade - Unicorn
Ted - Unicorn
Windooraa - The sorceress
Roy - The dragon
Gorgon – Lord Gorgon
Potts - The housekeeper
Quackmore - The housekeeper
Daniellah- The good witch
Vijjilanti - The Evil baddie
Cherrypee- The tree keeper
Cackles- The forest doctor
Flipflop - Bush hunter
Buttshot - Pumpkin killer
Nagem - the poo burier

Sofo Rox

Book one.

The book of Rox

Chapter 1. The Sneeze.

One hundred years ago, in a badly lit room, inside of Castle Rox. Cruella and Dabidee were busy working on a new potion from the Book of Rox.

Cruella and Dabidee were unicorn riders. They flew all the time with their unicorns Applejack, Ted, and Jade. Cruella and Dabidee loved the unicorns so much. The unicorns loved them too, but Cruella and Dabidee were always pimping, and the unicorns did not love that, because Unicorns have big noses.

Cruella and Dabidee were about to make a potion that would make their pimps smell like apples. The unicorns loved apples.

Cruella was adding cinnamon to the potion when a bit blew up Dabidee's nose and made her sneeze. She felt a snotter come out, but because the room was so badly lit, she didn't see where it went.

"Cover your mouth!" Cruella yelled. "Hurry up, turn the page. What's the next ingredient?"

"Geez, sorry!" Dabidee said as she turned the page. There was nothing else on the list.

"All finished," Dabidee said.

They both drank the potion.

Kabang! There was an explosion.

The unicorns started to cry. They could smell and taste pimps, but they weren't apple pimps. They were evil pimps.

The unicorns looked for Cruella and Dabidee, but they had both vanished along with the Book of Rox.

Chapter 2. Bourbonville and the Cloud Riders.

Bourbonville was a city in the clouds. It had lots of tall buildings, shops, and restaurants.

Right in the middle of Bourbonville was Castle Rox. You could see the castle from miles away. Unicorns used to live there a long time ago but not anymore. Now unicorns were grumpy and rude.

Nobody in Bourbonville had seen a happy unicorn in over a hundred years, and nobody knew why.

The people of Bourbonville had oversized ears, which came in handy when they were riding clouds. Cloud riding was fun. To ride a cloud, all they had to do is throw some cloud glitter on it, jump on, and flap their ears. Everyone loved it.

Bur and Twiggs were the best cloud riders in Bourbonville. They could do tricks and stunts, and their ears flapped so fast that they were almost invisible.

Today they were visiting Rhyco's cloud shop. Rhyco was a cloud genius. He knew everything about clouds. He knew how to clean them, fix them, and even how to fit them with Wi-Fi, which is what Bur and Twiggs were here for today.

"Can you give us Wi-Fi, Rhyco?" the riders asked.

"Sure can," Rhyco said. "It will take about an hour, so go grab some lunch, and I'll have it ready for when you get back."

Bur and Twiggs set off for Pandoo's restaurant.

Pandoo's was a fast-food joint that sold only pork chops.

"What will it be today?" Pandoo asked.

Bur and Twiggs smiled and said, "Do you have any pork chops?"

Pandoo smiled back and then yelled at the chef, "Porka chopa, pronto, pronto!"

Bur and Twiggs finished their chops, which were the best they ever had, and then said goodbye to Pandoo. Pandoo waved goodbye, happy that they loved his chops.

When Bur and Twigs got back to Rhyco's cloud shop, they had not only Wi-Fi but the shiniest clouds in Bourbonville. "Thanks Rhyco," they said as they flew off.

Chapter 3. The Goth Janny.

Kroxy Jnr was dressed head to toe in black. It was hot outside, but that didn't stop him from putting his hood up too.

He was busy cleaning the bins when three unicorns flew past and knocked over a row of bins.

"What's wrong with you? You wanna piece of me?" he shouted, and waved his fist about, then threw his best karate pose.

"That's enough of that, young man!" MizJojo said.

"But Mum, they are always trying to do me like that, always trying to ruin things. Why can't they just be nice? Who does that?" Kroxy Jnr said.

MizJojo smiled. "The unicorns used to be fun and friends with everyone. Nobody knows why they are grumpy now, but that doesn't mean you should be grumpy too. Now hurry up! You still have the toilet to clean—it's blocked again."

Kroxy Jnr sighed and closed his eyes. When he opened them up again, Penny the cheerleader jumped out in front of him singing,"

Hey Kroxy, show me that smile!

Gimme an S,

gimme an M,

gimme an I,

gimme an L,

gimme an E!

What do you get?"

Kroxy Jnr rolled his eyes and sulked off to the toilets.

MizJojo smiled at Penny. "Don't worry about him," she said. "He will smile later. Now let's go get some cake."

Penny cheered as they went off to the castle bakery.

Chapter 4. Glitter Run.

Sofo was busy at work in the laboratory at Castle Rox. Her dog, Floof, was by her side.

Sofo was a top scientist, the best in all of Bourbonville. She wore a white lab coat with four pens in her pocket and a pencil behind her ear. She took off her glasses to stare harder at the equation she was working on.

$$A+p>ll-e$$
$$=fu<n$$

"Oh, Floof, I just can't solve this. We need to figure out how to make the unicorns happy again. Everyone thinks they are grumpy, but I know they used to love people. We just have to find out what went wrong."

Floof put his big dog face on her leg and drooled a bit, then made a big bark. "Woof!"

Someone was at the door. It was Kroxalot, Sofo's dad.

"Would you like to go to the glitter farm with me? We are running low on cloud glitter," Kroxalot said.

Sofo sighed, then smiling admitted, "We could use the break."

She ran for the cloud, shouting "Shotgun! Come on, Floof, it's a glitter run."

Chapter 5. The Black Light.

Thirty-eight miles later, Sofo, Floof, and Kroxalot arrived at the glitter farm. It was beautiful, with hills of glitter in every colour as far as the eye could see.

"Ahoy there, what be having you?" called out Jimbob, the glitter boss. Jimbob used to be a pirate until he won money in a ping-pong tournament and bought a glitter farm with the winnings.

Kroxalot was talking to Jimbob about glitter when Sofo noticed Floof sniffing a pile of green and purple glitter. Floof dug up an old scrap of paper and gave it to Sofo.

It was a map.

Jimbob laughed. "Oh, not that old map. My old pal, Pee-Lee used to talk about it all the time. It's meant to take you to the Book of rox, but no matter how many people have searched for it, the book has not been seen in over 100 years"

"Can I have it?" Sofo asked.

"You sure can, but it might be a fake. Like I said, nobody has ever found the Book of Rox," Jimbob said.

"Hmm, I am an explorer. Let me see it," Kroxalot said.

He took out a black light from one of the twenty-seven pockets on his explorer's jacket.

"What are you doing?" Sofo asked.

"The best maps are hidden," Kroxalot replied.

He shone his black light on the map, and suddenly, another map came into view.

He pointed to an X on the newly revealed map. "Better make it your best glitter, Jimbob—we're going to the Badlands."

Chapter 6. The Badlands.

Sofo, Floof, and Kroxalot were flying in their clouds high above the Badlands.

It was a scary place. Volcanoes spat lava into the air and blocked out the sun. It was ridiculously hot, and the smell was enough to make you cry. It was an evil smell.

"Over there, that's the spot," said Kroxalot, pointing towards a big rock in the shape of an X.

They landed and set about digging.

Three hours and eighteen minutes later, the ground gave way, and they fell down a huge hole.

Everything went dark.

Kroxalot took out a bright yellow torch from one of his twenty-seven pockets.

The room was dusty, full of cobwebs and shadows, and right in the middle of the room was a book.

The Book of Rox!

Kroxalot couldn't believe it.

"My great-great-great-grandmother wrote this book. I've been looking for it my whole life," he said.

He went to pick up the book from the middle of the room. There was a noise from behind.

Someone else was in the room.

Somewhere from the dark, a net flew through the air and landed on Kroxalot, Sofo, and Floof. They fell to the floor.

Trapped.

Chapter 7. The Unlikely Hero.

Everyone was scared, scrambling around trying to get out of the net. Then a match was lit, and as the room started to glow, Sofo could see two women in front of her. It was Cruella and Dabidee, the Bourbonville witches.

"*Agghh!* What have I told you about lighting matches near me?" Cruella yelled.

"I'm sorry, I forgot again," Dabidee said.

Cruella and Dabidee stared at Sofo, Floof and Kroxalot, feeling angry, scared, and sad all at the same time. They had not seen another living person in over 100 years.

"Why have you come here?" Dabidee asked.

"It's useless, you can't help us!" Cruella said.

Cruella and Dabidee walked towards the door. Cruella stopped before going through. "Stupid people! Now you have to stay here too."

She closed the door tight behind her, locking Sofo, Floof, and Kroxalot inside.

The room got darker. Kroxalot's torch started to fade then went out.

"Quick, get another torch," Sofo said.

"I don't have another torch," Kroxalot said.

"Are you kidding me? Twenty-seven pockets, and no torch that actually works in the dark?" Sofo said.

Floof started to cry. He didn't like the dark.

Kroxalot tried to help by giving Floof hugs, but Sofo knew that was just because he was scared too.

Everything went quiet.

Then *bang*!

The door burst open. Once the dust settled, Sofo could see a crazy-looking woman. "Who are you"? she asked.

"My name is Handsome Dave. I am number one commando in all Japan."

"How did you get here?" Kroxalot asked.

"My Hot Air Balloon go too high; I get lost in the clouds. I crash here and find you. Can you help me get back to my platoon?" said Handsome Dave.

"Yeah, said Sofo, I mean *all* we have to do is deal with Cruella and Dabidee, *then* figure out how to get us all home on our clouds. Shouldn't be a problem" she said sarcastically.

"We will get you there Dave" said Kroxalot.

Sofo looked at Kroxalot, took a deep breath and said, "Pass me the Book of Rox".

Chapter 8. Apple pimps.

Kroxalot, Floof and Handsome Dave- the commando from Japan, were huddled together eating energy bars from the pockets of Kroxalots' explorers' jacket. "Fantastic! The pockets of Rox" said Handsome Dave.

Sofo was studying the Book of Rox. There was a bookmark at a potion called Apple pimps. After reading it a few times, Sofo said "I think I know why the Unicorns are grumpy. I think Cruella and Dabidee were trying to make their pimps smell like apples. They must have been Unicorn riders; everyone knows that Unicorns love apples".

Sofo showed them the Book of Rox and said "Here, look at the pages. Two of them are stuck together with some kind of green goo, but when you peel them apart there is another page to the potion. They missed a page!"

"What does that mean?" asked Kroxalot.

"I think Cruella and Dabidee missed a page of the potion and got it wrong. Instead of making Apple pimps they made some kind of Evil pimps. That's probably why the Badlands smell so bad" said Sofo.

"I hate Evil pimps" said Handsome Dave.

"Wait! Does that mean that Cruella and Dabidee are not really evil and we can make the Unicorns happy again?" said Kroxalot?

Sofo smiled then said, "Let's get to work".

Chapter 9. The Disco Ventriloquist.

Kroxy Jnr was in his hut. Everyone thought it was just a stinky old cupboard full of mops and things, but they were wrong.

From the ceiling hung a huge disco ball. The floor was made of giant neon squares that lit up when you stood on them. One wall was made up of TV screens that he used to monitor all the cloud cars in Bourbonville, and the other walls were covered in glass cases that held puppet dolls inside them.

Kroxy Jnr loved to disco dance. He couldn't sing that well, so he used puppet dolls to do the singing. Kind of like a ventriloquist. As he was dancing and making his puppet sing, he noticed a cloud on his monitor.

It was way outside of Bourbonville.

It was Kroxalot's cloud.

Kroxy Jnr used his radio to check in on Kroxalot, but there was no answer.

He was worried.

He spoke into his radio again.

This time to get help, and only the fastest help in Bourbonville would do.

Chapter 10. Fixing things right.

Cruella and Dabidee were in their Cave. They had been fighting and now they were both crying loudly.

The door to the cave creaked open and Sofo slowly walked in.

"*What are you doing here? Get her!*" yelled Dabidee. Cruella and Dabidee ran to grab Sofo, but Handsome Dave stopped them.

"I am Handsome Dave, Number one Commando in all Japan. Sofo wants to help you".

Cruella and Dabidee looked more confused than ever. "Help us? *Why?* Don't you know that it's our fault that the Unicorns don't like people anymore?" Said Dabidee.

"No, you made a mistake with your spell, look here". Sofo showed them the pages of the book that were stuck together and explained how they had missed ingredients and that they had made Evil pimps instead of Apple pimps.

Cruella and Dabidee looked at each other, then Cruella smacked Dabidee on the head and shouted, "*I told you to cover your mouth, you are always spraying snotters everywhere!*"

"Calm down, you'll hurt yourself again. We can fix things right, now that we know what went wrong poppet" said Dabidee. "We will need the unicorns here to fix things, but they won't want to come near us with their big noses" said Cruella.

"*Not a problem!* I will get the Unicorns. You stay here and fix that potion Sofo" said Kroxalot as he pulled a rope and gas masks from the Pockets of Rox, then he jumped onto his cloud and flew off in a flash.

Sofo worked with Cruella and Dabidee to make the new potion.

After a long time, it was ready.

Just at that same time Kroxalot arrived with three Unicorns tied to the back of his cloud. They were all wearing Gas masks.

"I got them, but I'm out of cloud dust now. We might need some help getting home" said Kroxalot.

"It's time" said Sofo as she handed the potion to Cruella and Dabidee. They both walked towards the Unicorns. "I hope this works" said Cruella. "Course it will, Poppet" said Dabidee.

Cruella and Dabidee closed their eyes and drank the potion all up.

At first, they looked shocked. Then their frowns started to fade, smiles started to form, and their eyes filled up with happy tears.

"I can smell apples" said handsome Dave.

"*I just done a pimp*" said Cruella, "*It's working! It's working*" said Dabidee, excitedly.

The Unicorns horns started to glow, then their whole body, and then in a huge colourful explosion- rainbows blew out their butts.

Cruella and Dabidee were hugging the unicorns and dancing.

"Well done Sofo! How can we ever thank you?" said Cruella.

Before Sofo could answer, Ted the Unicorn scooped her and Floof up on to his back and started to fly off towards Bourbonville. Applejack and Jade scooped up Cruella and Dabidee and they flew off too.

I am a Unicorn rider thought Sofo. She had a huge smile on her face as the wind rushed through her hair.

"*Weeeeeeeeeeeeee*".

Floof whimpered. He was scared and held on tight to Sofo.

Kroxalot looked at Handsome Dave and asked, "Do you know how to jump start a cloud?"

"I am Handsome Dave, number one commando in all Japan" said Handsome Dave.

Kroxalot sighed, then he smiled as two clouds zipped past him. It was Bur and Twiggs. "Fancy a ride on a real cloud?" Asked Bur.

Everyone got into the clouds. "Buckle up" said Twiggs.

Ears started to flap, the clouds started to shake, "To Bourbonville! yelled Kroxalot.

Chapter 11. The Altogether.

Bourbonville was alive with music from the parade.

Glitter and confetti cannons boomed and filled the sky with colour, making it extra pretty.

Bur, Twiggs and Rhyco were dancing while flying their clouds.

Jimbob was telling jokes to people on the street and setting off glitter cannons.

Pandoo was giving out free Pork Chops to everyone.

Handsome Dave was doing the robot dance while saying, "I am number one dancer in all japan".

Kroxy Jnr had his best puppet on his arm. He was singing and dancing, and he had on a multi coloured outfit for the first time ever. Penny cheered for him and he gave her a big smile.

Penny started cheering.

"He gave me a smile, he gave me a smile, he gave me a smile! *Go Kroxy!*"

Dabidee and Cruella were incredibly happy.

They had their best dresses on, and they were just back from the hairdressers and now they had hair cuts that looked like large pineapples.

Ted, Jade and Applejack flew around everyone as they danced in the air.

Dabidee and Cruella hugged Sofo and said, "Thank you for saving the unicorns and making us happy again".

MizJoJo hugged Kroxalot just as another glitter cannon went off.

As the glitter fell down over them, she gave him a romantic kiss.

Bourbonville was altogether again!

It was a great day.

Sofo felt so happy.

She gave Floof a big hug and said, "*What should we do for our next adventure?*"

The End

Sofo Rox.

Book two.

Alone in Bourbonville

Chapter 1. The beginning of Rox.

Five thousand years ago, deep in the clouds was the city of Buttingle.

Windooraa the sorceress was busy putting the final touches on a book that she had been working on for a long time. She swished her wand, and purple sparks shot out of the wand towards the book. Her wand was golden, and in the shape of a crowbar. Windooraa was binding the book with magic.

When she was finished, she sat the book upon a stand, in the middle of the room. The cover of the book read- The Book of Rox.

Windooraa gave a smile to her Dragon that lay by the fire, happy that she was finished at last. She swished her crowbar wand once more and said, "The Book of Rox will always work its magic to help people, when they need it".

Behind Windooraa, her husband Gorgon was climbing on a chair, trying to sneak into the biscuit tin. The Dragon was watching him and flicked its tail, snapping one of the chair legs. The chair wibbled and wobbled, causing Gorgon to fall off, bashing his head on the floor.

Chapter 2. Everyone is using it.

Back in Bourbonville, a lot had changed since the Book of Rox had been found. The people of Bourbonville used its magic all the time. It was fun and made things quicker.

Cruella and Dabidee used it to get themselves new party frocks.

Bur and Twiggs used it to upgrade their cloud cars.

Jimbob got a new glitter tractor with the licence plate PL33, to remind him of his old pal Pee-Lee.

Penny used it to make pom poms that had speakers built into the handles, so that she had music to dance to while she cheered.

Pandoo used it to create a new pork flavoured pork chop called Pandoopork.

Rhyco used it to make a games room in his garage.

Kroxy Jnr used it to pimp-out his disco room with voice activated dance floor lights.

MizJojo used it to get unlimited clothes from PrimRox, her favourite clothes shop.

Kroxalot used it to get new tools for his jacket that had 27 pockets on it, and Handsome Dave used it to learn how to street dance, now that there was nobody left to fight.

Sofo and Floof were the only ones that had not used the book yet.

Floof wanted to use it to make squirrels run slower, but Sofo wouldn't let him.

"Don't be lazy Floof. Remember, scientists don't cut corners, we figure things out-without magic" said Sofo.

Floof sighed, then went back to work with Sofo.

Chapter 3. Too busy today.

Sofo and Floof had been working hard all week and decided to go see their friend Handsome Dave. When they got to Handsome Dave's caravan, they found Dave dancing outside on the grass.

"Looking good Dave. Do you want to go into town for lunch?" asked Sofo.

"*Too busy!* Now that I have nobody to fight, I become number 1 street dancer in all Japan" Said Handsome Dave.

Dave's a bit rude, thought Sofo as she left.

Sofo went to see the Unicorns, Applejack, Ted, and Jade. "Hi everyone, do you want to do something together today?" asked Sofo.

Jade was playing a kazoo, badly and did not hear Sofo.

Ted was chasing a Fox around the garden and did not see Sofo. Applejack was trying to trim his mane while looking into a tiny mirror. He grumped as he made a bald patch by mistake. "Not today, I have to fix my hair".

How rude, thought Sofo as she left.

Sofo and Floof went to see Mizjojo and Kroxalot, but they were rude too.

Kroxalot was playing with one of his tools in his 27-pocket jacket, and Mizjojo was busy trying on more clothes. They didn't even notice that Sofo and Floof were there to see them.

"What's wrong with everyone?" said Sofo as she walked off with Floof, feeling a little upset

Chapter 4. Alone in Bourbonville.

Two weeks had past and Sofo had tried to meet all her family and friends, but they were all too busy. At first Sofo felt hurt, but she soon noticed it wasn't just her that they had no time for. Everyone was too busy to see anyone.

They were all too busy with the things they had gotten from the Book of Rox.

Too busy to spend time with people.

"This isn't right Floof, they can't go on like this. Nobody is spending time together anymore, and now they have stopped talking too!" said Sofo.

Feeling sad, she jumped face first into her huge, galaxy coloured beanbag.

Chapter 5. The town fight.

The next day Sofo and Floof set off to castle Rox to see if they could use the Book of Rox to fix things.

"I hope we can use the book to help everyone Floof. They have all forgotten about each other, and I know they are always happiest when they are all together" said Sofo.

On the way to the castle, Sofo and Floof met lots of people.

Dabidee and Cruella were arguing "*I can't believe you shrank all of my lovely costumes!*" Yelled Dabidee who was wearing a teeny, tiny, itty-bitty Cinderella costume, which did not cover her bottom properly. "*Well at least you didn't get caught pimpin on a video chat*" screeched Cruella." *You are always pimpin*" growled Dabidee. They both ignored Sofo as they angrily stomped off towards the castle.

Jimbob was laughing at Applejack. "That magic shaver is definitely wonky. *Your hair looks like a badger*" he said. Applejack was not happy, and they both ignored Sofo and Floof as they headed towards castle Rox.

Jade had swallowed her Kazoo and now sounded like a tired-out duck, and Ted was absolutely stinking. "I can't believe my luck, who slips in Fox poo?" Said Ted. "*Quack*" said a worried looking Jade.

Kroxy Jnr was carrying a broken piece of his Disco floor under his arm. His face was really red, and he was muttering "lights on! What's so hard to understand about that?"

Sofo walked past Rhyco's cloud shop and saw him shaking his head at a broken games chair. He gave it a kick and yelped "*Ouch!*" as his foot hit the metal frame of the chair.

Pandoo was walking along the street crying into a big yellow hankie. "It's gone. *Gone!* I've lost my Pandoopork recipe, no more porkachoppa, *whaaaaa*".

Twiggs had been drinking dizzy juice and Bur was crying about a greenie that had been hanging out of her nose during a video chat that had now gone viral.

Sofo noticed that Twiggs still had her slippers on, so she tried to tell her, but Twiggs did not listen.

At castle Rox, Mizjojo was furious. "*Banned! They have banned me from PrimRox!*" She shouted at Kroxalot.

Kroxalot was struggling to stay standing. The weight of all the tools in his jacket with 27 pockets was making it too heavy for him to stay standing up, and he fell backwards to the ground.

Everyone was so angry, that they hadn't noticed that they were all at the castle to use the Book of Rox at the same time, and of course, everyone wanted to use it first.

A huge fight broke out.

Sofo and Floof tried to get them to stop fighting but nobody listened. She knew she had to do something, but she didn't know what. She grabbed the Book of Rox while everyone was fighting and ran off to her laboratory to try and figure out how to put things right again.

Chapter 6. Broken.

Sofo was back in her laboratory, studying the book. "We need to figure this out. Why is everyone fighting, and why is everything that the book gave them, now not working?" She asked Floof.

Floof was now glad that he hadn't used the book to make Squirrels slower. He thought to himself, what if the book had made Squirrels faster?

Sofo got out her super-smart, scientific magnifying glass to inspect the book. She could not see anything that looked broken, but she did find two small inscriptions that she hadn't noticed before, on the back of the book.

The Book of Rox will always work its magic to help people, when they need it.

Bound in magic by Windooraa.
Buttingle city BV1 R78

"We need to take the book and find Windooraa, maybe she can help
us fix everything. We have to try. Bourbonville isn't fun anymore.
Quick Floof, get the map we're going to Buttingle" said Sofo.

Chapter 7. Buttingle and the Sorceress.

Sofo and Floof had been flying in their cloud car for eleven hours and twenty-three minutes when they finally got to Buttingle.

The clouds in Buttingle were not fluffy and airy like the ones in Bourbonville, they were hot, thick and hard to pass through.

They landed beside an old house.

When they got to the door, a sign on it read.

Windooraa the Sorceress

 The door opened on its own. Sofo and Floof were a little scared but they went inside, and the door creaked to a close behind them. Tiny wings without bodies fluttered around them, landing on their shoulders, and then took their jackets from them and hung them on the wall by the door. "You look like you could use a nice cup of tea" said a voice coming from the back of the room.

A woman stepped forward. She was wearing a purple cloak with yellow stars on it and a blue hat with black circles. In her right hand she was clasping a golden crowbar.

"My name is Windooraa. Pleased to meet you".

Chapter 8. Coming together.

Everyone had stopped fighting and had calmed down a bit at castle Rox.

The great hall was a mess. Tables had been turned over and chairs had been smashed.

Curtains and pictures had been ripped from the walls and were now in a pile on the floor.

Kroxy Jnr was rubbing his head, where Penny the cheerleader had hit him with her pom poms, breaking the speakers in the handles.

Kroxalot took off his jacket with the 27 pockets, and all at once he felt better.

Mizjojo put down her last PrimRox bag, then she felt better too.

Everyone started to put down the things that the Book of Rox had gave them, the things that were now not working.

They all felt much better.

"Where's Sofo and Floof?" asked Mizjojo.

"Quick, Kroxy Jnr, check your cloudcam app" said Kroxalot.

Kroxy Jnr checked the app on his phone and found Sofo's cloud. "It says they are in a place called Buttingle?" said Kroxy Jnr.

Kroxalot looked worried. "I've been to Buttingle a long time ago. It is not a safe place! We need to go and bring them back home before anything bad happens to them."

Chapter 9. Crowbars can't fly.

Windooraa and Sofo had been talking for a while now. Sofo had told her all about Bourbonville, The Book of Rox and that everyone was now fighting.

Floof had passed out, asleep on the floor, after Windooraa had gave him a ham-bag to eat.

Windooraa nodded her head and said,

"I was the one that bound the Book of Rox in magic for your great, great, great Grandfather. Such a silly man. I sealed it with magic, and it cannot break. Its impossible!

The book of Rox will always work its magic to help people, when they need it".

"Can you come back with me to Bourbonville to help fix everything with your magic?" asked Sofo.

"I wish I could, but your cloud only has room for you and Floof, and Lord Gorgon has taken my magic Dragon, so I can't fly anywhere" said Windooraa.

Sofo did not want to give up, so she asked, "Can't you use your magic Crowbar to fly?"

"No. It's the only thing my wand cannot do. Crowbars cannot fly, even magic ones.

Windooraa felt sad now. She looked down at the floor and said "I miss my Dragon; his name is Roy, I used to fly everywhere with him.

Sofo was thinking over everything that Windooraa had told her, and she was now confused. "Wait! who is Lord Gorgon?" Asked Sofo.

Chapter 10. Lord Gorgon.

Lord Gorgon walked through the Dungeon halls of his castle in Buttingle.

He wore a black cape, with red flowing lines through it, and a huge, big bandage on his head. He had a biscuit wrapper stuck under his shoe and it made a scrunchy noise as he walked.

"Potts! Quackmore! Get in here!" he yelled at the top of his voice.

Potts and Quackmore rushed down the hall towards him and both said in harmony "Yes Lord Gorgon, what is your command?"

"Clean the dragons cage, and will you please stop feeding him curry. The smell in here is spoiling my good mood. Now, where is my tea and biscuits?" he bawled, this time even louder.

"Sorry, Lord Gorgon, yes Lord Gorgon, we will fix it Lord Gorgon" said Potts, rushing off to clean the Dragons cage, while Quackmore went to fetch the tea and biscuits.

Lord Gorgon stood by the fireplace, rubbing his head.

"My poor head, all I want is some peace and quiet. They just don't make servants like they used to" he said as he pulled a secret biscuit out from behind a picture frame and munched into it. "Quackmore! Tea! Now!" he screeched.

Chapter 11. Wanted in forty-two states.

Windooraa was telling Sofo about Lord Gorgon. "He's my husband. He isn't actually a Lord. About 5000 years ago, while I was sealing the Book of Rox with magic, he bumped his head. I bandaged him up, then I went to find a spell to heal him, but when I came back, he had vanished, along with My Dragon Roy and our house keepers Potts and Quackmore. I think the bump gave him amnesia because he does not remember who he is anymore. I have not been able to find him in all this time. I have tried to, but because I put a magic bandage on his head, my wand can't find him. He must still have the bandage on.

I have read about him a few times. He must think he is an evil Lord now. He keeps breaking into Biscuit factory's and looting their biscuits. He is now wanted in forty-two states.

I have tried to go find him whenever I hear that he has robbed another factory, but I am always too late. He is always gone by the time I get there. So, now I just wait here in the hope that one day he takes off the bandage, and I can find him or that he remembers who he really is and comes home on his own.

I miss him".

Sofo felt that she had to cheer Windooraa up so she said "I can't believe that you were there when the Book of Rox was made. That is amazing. Don't worry, My Dad is an explorer. He will help us find Lord Gorgon. We just need to figure out how to get us all to Bourbonville first".

Chapter 12. Dead end.

Kroxalot and Kroxy Jnr sped through the air in their cloud car, closely followed by Twiggs, Bur, Rhyco and Jimbob. They circled around the entrance to Buttingle. Just off to the west they saw a castle ruin. "Let's check there" said Kroxalot.

They parked their clouds by the castle ruins and started to look for Sofo and Floof. They had been inside the castle for twenty-eight and a half minutes when they heard a huge growl from behind.

"Potts! Quackmore! We have trespassers again; they are trying to steal my biscuits!

Lock them up or feed them to the Dragon but be quiet. It's my biscuit time!" shrieked Lord Gorgon. Suddenly, the wall behind them crashed down, revealing a humongous dragon!

Terrified, they all ran into the next room, but it was a dead end.

Slam! The door closed behind them. They were trapped.

Chapter 13. Two skooshes of hair spray.

"Oh, I just can't wait to find out how my wee poppets are. I'm just so worried about Sofo and Floof. I miss their wee faces" said Dabidee. "Me too, there's only one thing to do, let's get the cauldron out, and find them the old-fashioned way" said Cruella.

Dabidee scuttled off to get the cauldron from the basement, while Cruella fetched an old spell book from the attic. She blew the dust off it, and it made her cough, and a squidgy pimp snuck out at the same time.

They started to add things into the cauldron. Cruella called out ingredients and Dabidee plopped them in the cauldron and stirred them with a whopping big wooden spoon.

"Radish and a yellow toenail" – *Plop, plop, Stir.*

"Beaver hair and pickled wasps" *Plop, plop, stir.*

"Shredded pants"

"No chance! You can put them in yourself" Dabidee grumbled. "Just hurry up and do it" quipped Cruella.

Plop, plop, stir.

"Time for the last ingredient please, a jar of Air du'bum" said Cruella. Dabidee took a jar from under her cloak and plopped it into the cauldron and gave it a good stir. Cruella pushed Dabidee out the way and added 2 skooshes of hairspray into the cauldron, and the water turned into a clear looking glass.

"I see them. Oh, there they are, my wee dears. Look, they are with someone in a purple outfit" said Dabidee.

"*Shhh*, I'm trying to see" said Cruella.

"Well, I never. That's Windooraa. She is the most powerful sorceress that ever lived. I thought she was dead. She has been missing for about 5000 years.

Quick, go get help Dabidee. I'll see if I can find Kroxalot too" said Cruella.

Alone in Bourbonville.

Chapter 14. War Paint.

Kroxy Jnr was kicking the door of the Dungeon that Potts and Quackmore had locked them in.

"Please stop Kroxy Jnr. Didn't you hear what they said- they will feed us to the Dragon!" cried Twiggs.

Bang!

Stop it!" said Bur.

"That wasn't me" said Kroxy Jnr.

Bang!

Bang!

The door burst open, flying off its hinges, causing dust to fill the room. Standing where the door used to be, with a face covered in war paint was Handsome Dave.

"I am Handsome Dave, number one commando in all Japan.

"*Yes!*" they all cheered.

"How did you get here?" asked Kroxy Jnr.

"He flew with me" said Rhyco, who had just walked into the dungeon, feeling like a hero.

"*Yes!*" They all cheered and hugged.

"Let's go, we need to find Sofo and Floof and get back to Bourbonville" said Kroxalot.

Chapter 15. New Friends.

"This place is like a maze" said Kroxy Jnr. "Yeah, who would build a castle like this? It's in ruins. Who does that?" asked Rhyco.

"Not us" said two voices from behind, in harmony.

Handsome Dave jumped in front of everyone to protect them, in a Kung-Fu like pose.

"Wait! We want to help you" the two voices said together.

"Who are you?" asked Handsome Dave.

"I am Potts, and this is Quackmore. We want to help you" said Potts.

"What about that Dragon? How do we know you are not trying to trick us and feed us to it?" said Rhyco.

"No, no, don't worry about him. His name is Roy, and he prefers macaroni with apples, he is just a bit loud and clumsy. We can show you the way out, but please take us, and Roy with you. We need to find Windooraa, she can fix Lord Gorgon" said Quackmore.

"Fine, just show us the way out. We have to find Sofo and Floof" said Twiggs.

Potts and Quackmore said, "We haven't met Sofo or Floof yet, but when we find Windooraa, she will help you".

Potts and Quackmore carefully started to lead everyone out of castle Buttingle.

They heard Lord Gorgon yelling *"Potts! Quackmore! Get the Dragon. The prisoners have escaped"*. "Hurry, he's coming" said Potts and Quackmore."

Chapter 16. The learner pigeon.

Sofo, Floof and Windooraa were in the garden. Sofo was trying to suggest ideas about how they could get back to Bourbonville.

"I'm sorry my dear, my crowbar can't fly, and I have to stay here in case Lord Gorgon remembers who he is and comes home" Said Windooraa.

Sofo turned away feeling deflated. She looked up in the sky, then started to smile.

She could see Cruella and Dabidee on their Unicorns, Ted and Jade. They landed and rushed straight to hug Sofo and Floof. "Oh poppets, I've just missed you so much. You gave us all a rare fright" said Dabidee.

When Cruella had finished hugging them, she walked towards Windooraa and said, "hello old friend, it's good to see you again".

"Yes, it's been rather a while, hasn't it?" said Windooraa.

"Wait, what? You two know each other?" asked Sofo.

Windooraa nodded, "yes, we used to shave unicorns together at the racetrack".

"That was before you became the most powerful sorceress around" said Cruella.

"As I remember, we were the best Unicorn shavers in town" said Windooraa, winking.

Sofo got excited. "This is great, now we can all go home to Bourbonville" she said.

Windooraa shook her head. "I'm sorry my dear, but there's still not enough room on your cloud and I see only two unicorns, and I still need to wait for Lord Gorgon".

"*Neigh, Neigh, Stupid pigeon*" groaned Applejack, who was flying towards them fast, landing on the ground with a thud. He shook his mane. There was a big bit missing and it looked like a badger's haircut. "Sorry I am late. I got stuck behind a learner Pigeon. Now, who needs a lift?" he said.

Sofo Turned to Windooraa.

Windooraa shook her head again and said, "I'm sorry Sofo, I really want to come and help you all, but I must wait here in case Lord Gorgon returns".

Cruella put her hand on Windooraa's shoulder and said "Don't worry about that, I know exactly where he is. I found him in the cauldron looking glass, and he is with Kroxalot too".

Windooraa shone with a purple light, and with a flip of her crowbar wand she zapped herself onto Applejacks back. "Top speed, if you would be so kind Mr. Jack,

Let's go".

Chapter 17. Reunited.

Just as Kroxalot was coming out of castle Buttingle, he saw Sofo's cloud heading towards them. He was both pleased and worried at the same time. He didn't want that dragon to eat her, or Lord Gorgon to take her Prisoner. Buttingle was a dangerous place he thought.

Applejack landed and a woman dressed in purple zapped straight off his back and appeared right in front of Kroxalot. "Hello, I'm Windooraa. Pleased to meet you. Now, if you don't mind, take me to Lord Gorgon" She said.

"No way! He has a dragon chasing us, and he tried to lock us up" said Kroxalot.

"Don't worry about the Dragon, Roy loves Windooraa" said Potts and Quackmore as they ran forward to hug her. Potts and Quackmore told Windooraa everything that had happened. Windooraa said "alright, don't worry. I'm here now, I've missed you both so much".

Whack! Out of nowhere Lord Gorgon sucker punched Kroxalot, knocking him to the ground. Lord Gorgon took out his sword and raised it high above his head, then threw it down fast, towards Kroxalot.

Clang!

Purple sparks were flying out of Windooraa's crowbar wand as it blocked the sword from striking Kroxalot.

"That's enough of that" said Windooraa, pointing her wand at Lord Gorgon's head. He floated up in the air and started to spin around. As he spun, the dirty old bandage on his head started to disappear, then he gently fell back to the ground.

"That's your great, great, great grandson you were about to kill" Windooraa said to him.

Lord Gorgon was stunned. "Windooraa? Is that you? What's going on? Where are we?" asked Lord Gorgon.

Windooraa smiled and gave him a hug. "You hit your head, you daft brush. You have a lot of explaining to do with the biscuit factory, but we can deal with that later.

Right now, we must go and help put things right in Bourbonville. Step aside please, I will be flying with Roy today" she said, then zapped herself on to Roy's back. With another quick flick of her wand, she zapped Lord Gorgon on to Applejack, and they all flew off to Bourbonville.

Alone in Bourbonville.

Chapter 18. Together again.

Back in Bourbonville, everyone was together again.

Pandoo had organised a huge BBQ for everyone, all pork of course. Roy the dragon and Floof were most pleased by this.

Kroxy Jnr and Rhyco were making sure that everyone had drinks. Twiggs was playing music, while Bur, Penny and Handsome Dave danced with Potts and Quackmore.

Cruella and Dabidee were telling everyone about how they found Sofo by using their Air Du'bum potion.

Jade, Applejack and Ted were shooting magic rainbows out of their bottoms, while Jimbob was lifting glitter canons off his tractor.

Kroxalot was introducing Lord Gorgon to Mizjojo. "It's a pleasure to meet you" said Lord Gorgon.

Bourbonville was always at its best when everyone was together, thought sofo with a smile.

Chapter 19. Team Rox.

Sofo was pleased that everyone was together again, and that they were having fun, but she was worried about something.

"What's wrong Sofo?" asked Windooraa.

"Nothing, it's just, I'm worried that the Book of Rox still isn't working" said Sofo.

Windooraa smiled and then asked, "Isn't it?"

"What do you mean?" asked Sofo.

"The Book of Rox will always work its magic to help people, when they need it" said Windooraa.

"But it didn't work. Everyone got lazy and stopped talking to each other" said Sofo.

Windooraa smiled again.

Sofo was starting to get frustrated, "Why are you smiling?" she asked, impatiently.

Windooraa looked at her then said, "When everyone got lazy and stopped talking to each other, The Book stopped working. That sounds like a magic book to me.

When everyone started fighting and you could not get them to stop, you stole the book and brought it to me. Have you ever stolen a book before?"

"No! I have never stolen anything in my life! I promise" said Sofo.

"Windooraa held Sofo's hand and said, "Then that sounds to me, like something only a magic book could make you do.

Windooraa started to glow- purple, blue and pink.

"When you found me after all these years, did you know how lonely I was, or how much Lord Gorgon needed help?"

"No" said Sofo, feeling puzzled.

Windooraa smiled again and said "I bound the book in magic, and it cannot break. The Book of Rox will always work its magic for people, when they need it.

I believe the book knew that the people of Bourbonville needed each other, more than they needed the book. It stopped working because they didn't need it.

I believe that the book knew that you couldn't stop everyone from fighting, and that it had to be you to take the book, because only an explorer with a super- smart, scientific magnifying glass could find me.

I believe the book knew that Lord Gorgon, Potts, Quackmore, Roy and I, all needed your help, just as much as you needed ours. I believe the book done exactly what it was meant to do. It worked its magic for people, *when they needed it*.

Sofo was speechless.

Windooraa looked at everyone in Castle Rox, then asked "What do you see Sofo?"

Sofo looked at them. They were smiling, they were happy, they were together.

She couldn't speak and felt like she was going to burst with happiness.

Windooraa hugged her, just as Jimbob set off a glitter canon, filling the castle with sparkling colours.

"I see, Team Rox" said Sofo.

The end.

"Wait, if Lord Gorgon was there with you when you made the Book of Rox and Lord Gorgon is my great, great, great grandad, does that make you my...?

Windooraa hugged Sofo again before she could finish speaking and said.

"It's a magic book isn't it!'

Sofo Rox

Book three.

Sofo and the Shadow-Witch

Sofo

and the

Shadow witch

Sofo and the shadow-witch.

Chapter 1. It's ready.

Long, long ago, in Bourbonville, two women were busy making something. Working as fast as they could.

"Do you think this will work?"

"It has to. It's our only option. We have to save Bourbonville".

Sitting on a big wooden table, was a brand-new red case.

"It's ready".

Chapter 2. Hide n' seek.

"They will never find us in here Floof. Ha-ha we are the best at hide n' seek in all of Bourbonville" Said Sofo, as they ran through the grounds of castle Rox.

They ran past the drawbridge and headed to the east tower, then snuck inside the entrance to the old dungeon. The dungeon had been boarded up for years. This is the best hiding place ever, thought Sofo, super pleased with herself.

Twiggs and Bur had been watching Sofo and Floof. They had seen them go into the old dungeon. "Got you this time!" said Twiggs. "Yeah! Now we will be the hide n' seek champs" said Bur.

They ran to the dungeon door and went in to catch Sofo and Floof.

Sofo and Floof were inside the dungeon when they heard the door creek open, and footsteps coming their way.

"Huh? How did they know we were in here? Come on Floof, hide!" said Sofo.

They ran to a different room, looking for a new place to hide.

"Quick, through here" said Sofo, as she ran through an old wooden door.

The room was empty, apart from some old, rusted torture chains on the wall. They stood still, trying not to make a sound that would give away their new hiding place.

This bit of the castle is spooky thought Sofo. The shadows in the room looked scary, and her eyes were playing tricks on her. She took a deep breath and said to herself "Stay calm, it's only shadows."

Sofo felt the room turn icy cold, as a shadow moved from the corner of the room towards them.

It was a woman.

The woman was dressed like a witch, wearing a purple hood. Sofo couldn't see her face, only two bright red eyes that burned in the dark. The shadow slowly lifted its hand, it was holding a red case.

The shadow slowly opened the red case, and Sofo and Floof were sucked into the case in a flash of light.

The shadow slowly faded back into the corner and disappeared.

Twiggs and Bur were almost blinded by a flash of light as they ran through the door to catch Sofo and Floof.

"What was that?" said Bur.

"It must have been Sofo with her torch" said Twiggs.

They went into the room to catch them, but it was empty.

"That's weird, I'm sure I saw them go in here "said Bur.

"Come on, they must have snuck into another room "said Twiggs.

They looked for Sofo and Floof, but they were nowhere to be seen.

Hours passed.

"I'm really worried" said Twiggs.

"Me too, we need to get help" said Bur.

Twiggs and Bur ran off as fast as they could, to get help.

Chapter 3. The shadow-witch.

Sofo and Floof were on the ground, covering their eyes from the flash of light. As It faded away, Sofo rubbed her knee, she had hurt it on the ground. "Ouch, where are we Floof?" she said.

Floof whimpered, as she looked around.

They were in the middle of what looked like castle Rox, but this was not castle Rox.

This was a dark, spooky castle.

Some of the walls were missing and the roof above was gone.

"Where are we Floof"?

Floof ran and hid between Sofo's legs.

Sofo and Floof were cold.

They started to move through the castle ruins. Sofo felt like she knew this place, but she had never been here before. It gave her a spooky feeling.

They were walking towards the castle grounds when Sofo froze.

The shadow Witch was in front of them. Floating in the air. Its face hidden in shadow, with eyes, like red fires.

Sofo summoned all her courage and called out.

"Who are you?

Why have you brought us here?

What do you want?"

The shadow-witch slowly lifted its hand. Holding up a red case. Then floated backwards towards the forest.

Sofo and Floof were really scared. "I wish Team Rox were here Floof. Come on, we have to find a way home, and it looks like the shadow Witch is the only one that knows how to do that" said Sofo.

The pair followed the shadow-witch into the dark forest.

Chapter 4. Bourbonville.

Kroxalot was trying on his Halloween costume in the great hall. "I'm going to be amazing in this, just wait till they see me" he said, lovingly, to the mirror.

Crash!

Twiggs, and Bur burst into the great hall, knocking over a vase.

"Kroxalot, we can't find Sofo and Floof!" they yelled.

"I know, she really is good at hide n' seek. Taught her myself. Did you know I was hide n' seek champ for 13 years before retiring undefeated?" He said.

"No Kroxalot, it's not hide n' seek. This is different, she has been missing for hours" said Bur.

"We haven't seen them since they went into the old dungeon" said Twiggs.

Windooraa had been enjoying a nice cup of lemon and raspberry tea in the great hall when Twiggs and Bur had burst in.

"Kroxalot, I told you to seal the dungeon. It's not safe, it's full of dark spirits" she said scowling at him.

Windooraa turned to the girls and said, "Now, girls- tell me everything!"

Twiggs and Bur told Windooraa what they had seen.

Windooraa was silent and her face looked pale with worry.

When she eventually spoke, her voice was sharp.

"Kroxalot. Get a search party. Now!"

Chapter 5. Run Floof.

Sofo and Floof were following the shadow-Witch into the forest. The Witch had disappeared into a patch of trees up ahead that looked like Floof's favourite place in Bourbonville, but this was not Bourbonville. This was a dark, spooky place.

"We need to find the shadow-witch Floof, she's our only way home" said Sofo.

Snap! Came a noise from the forest.

"What was that?" asked Sofo.

Crunch!

Sofo and Floof were really scared. Their hearts were beating so fast, it was all they could hear as they scanned the forest, looking to find where the noises were coming from and who was making them.

Rooaarrr!

A huge, eleven-foot black bear charged through the bushes, straight at Sofo and Floof.

"Run Floof!" yelled Sofo.

Floof didn't need to be told twice. He flew ahead, and Sofo ran behind him.

Sofo jumped over a rock and bashed her head on a branch of a tree. Her head felt like it was burning as she ran.

The bear was closer now, swiping branches away with its huge claws and snarling at them with its enormous jaws.

They both kept running until they came to a dead-end.

The bear slowed down. Knowing they had no escape.

It stalked towards them, snarling.

Sofo hugged Floof, fearing that this was the end, and they were both about to become dinner. She thought of her friends in Bourbonville and closed her eyes.

Weeooweet!

A loud whistle came from somewhere nearby.

The bear stopped still when it heard the whistle.

Sofo could not believe her eyes. From the forest, a tree walked towards the bear, and with a swipe of a huge branch like arm, it threw the bear away, high over the treetops.

Stunned, Sofo and Floof were staring at the tree.

From behind it, came a group of forest people.

Chapter 6. The forest people.

Sofo and Floof were staring at the forest people, thinking- are they good or evil.

"Alright troops. Don't worry, we mean you no harm. My names Cherrypee. I am the tree keeper. This is Albert, my tree friend that just took care of your bear problem" said Cherrypee.

Cherrypee had mud all over his hands and face. He was wearing an old hat, and his curly hair was popping through the holes in it.

Sofo could tell that they were friendly and said "Thank you Cherrypee, my names Sofo and this is Floof. Pleased to meet you."

A woman stepped forward from beside Albert the tree.

"Come here my dears, I'm Cackles, the forrest doctor. Let me look at that nasty cut on your head."

Sofo's head was still sore from when she had banged it on a branch.

Cackles was nice, a little weird looking, but nice. She was wearing a plunger as a hat, and she had her hair in buns, either side of the plunger. She took out a pouch from her bag and set about fixing the cut on Sofo's head. "There all done" she said when she was finished.

"Let me introduce the rest of the family" said Cherrypee. This is Flipflop, our bush hunter". Flipflop was covered in mud and leaves and looked just like a bush, except his green, white and yellow - mow hawk hair. "Nice to meet you" said Flipflop.

"This is Buttshot" said Cherrypee.

A young man with red hair, white eyeshadow and blue eye liner, shook Sofo's hand.

"I kill pumpkins, Vermin that they are. One kick, straight to the Butt, and it's all over" Said Buttshot.

"And this is Nagem" said Cherrypee.

Nagem was beautiful thought Sofo. She had turquoise hair, black leggings, shiny boots and a nice eye patch.

"Hi, I'm Nagem- the poo burier. I bury poo's before the bears and pumpkins smell them. Do you need a poo?" She asked Sofo.

"Eh, no. I'm ok for now. Sofo said embarrassed, then asked, "Do you live here?"

"yeah, course we do. Have done since we came here long, long ago. Welcome to Pumpkinville" said Cherrypee.

"Long, long ago? Wow that is a long time. Where did you live before coming here then?" asked Sofo.

Cherrypee started twitching. His face turned purple and he was muttering something.

"There, there, calm down love" Cackles said to him, as she sat him down on Alberts trunk.

"Sorry Sofo, he doesn't like to talk about where we used to live. It makes him a bit upset, but I can tell you all about it if you like? I like to tell stories about it" Smiled Cackles.

Cackles described their old home to Sofo.

"It was full of rainbows, fluffy clouds, flying unicorns and happy people. Happy people that would sing with each other, have fun, and cared for each other" said Cackles.

Sofo was confused.

"If you don't mind me asking, why did you move here then?

It's dark and spooky here, and why are Pumpkins and bears trying to attack us?" Said Sofo.

Cherrypee stood up.

"We didn't move here.

Long, long ago there was a huge battle with a terrible evil. We got caught up in the middle of a magic spell and we were brought here by mistake. You're right Sofo, this is a dark spooky place, but sometimes it reminds me of home too" said Cherrypee.

Sofo wasn't sure what to say, but she wanted to help.

"Floof and me are looking for the shadow-Witch.

She brought us here in a red case, maybe she can help us all get home too.

The forest people went quiet, then Nagem said "The Shadow-Witch can't help Sofo.

There is no way back home. You should stay with us."

Sofo shook her head and said, "There must be away back. Floof and I will find away, and we will help you get back home too. Don't lose hope. Where is your home?" she asked.

Cherrypee was looking up at the sky, trying to find the stars.

"Bourbonville" he whispered.

Chapter 7. Sector three.

The search party was underway. Everyone was rushing around trying to find Sofo and Floof, or at least for a clue that could help find them.

"Aw me, am just soo feart for ma wee poppets.

Lost all on their own" said Dabidee.

"Agreed!" said Cruella.

Kroxalot had set up a search control board and was marking off areas that had been searched. "Sector two- negative" he said as he scored it off the list.

Mizjojo scowled at him. "Really? Sector two? Can't you just say upstairs like a normal person?"

Kroxalot gave her a hug and said "Don't worry, we will find them soon. Now, you go take Cruella and Dabidee and search Sector three".

"And where is sector three?" asked Mizjojo.

"The dungeon" said Jimbob as he put on his tennis bat-shoes, then said "I'm coming too".

Mizjojo, Cruella, Dabidee and Jimbob quickly got to sector three.

"Oh, I don't like it here, it's so dark and creepy, and would you just look at the décor. This place needs a makeover" said Dabidee.

They found the room that Twiggs and Bur had described, but it was empty.

Just as they were about to leave, Mizjojo screamed.

Arrrghhh!

A shadow was coming out of the wall towards them.

The shadow looked like a floating Witch, with Red eyes.

It slowly held up a red case, then in a flash, they were sucked into the case.

The shadow slowly faded back into the wall from where it came.

Chapter 8. The Pumpkin army.

Sofo was busy helping Nagem bury poo after dinner.

"This is really weird. Can pumpkins really smell poo, and why are they attacking us?" she asked.

"It's not weird, and they can. The pumpkins are the worst.

They are the Witches soldiers, and they are always trying to kill us Sofo.

Cherrypee says that the Witch has an army of pumpkins- Ten thousand strong.

That is why we call this place, Pumpkinville.

Burying poo is a dirty Job, but it is the only way to hide from the Pumpkins" Said Nagem.

Suddenly there was a flash of light, and then MizJojo, Jimbob, Cruella and Dabidee were standing in front of Sofo.

They all hugged.

"What's that smell?" asked Dabidee.

"It wasn't me; I'm wearing my shreddies!" said Cruella.

Floof was running circles around them, so happy to see them.

"How did you get here?" asked Sofo.

"I think it was a Witch" said Cruella.

"Yeah, a wee floaty purple one" said Dabidee.

"Don't worry, we have each other. Now, let's find a way back home" said Mizjojo.

Chapter 9. Negative.

Kroxalot was starting to worry.

All sectors were coming back as negative, and Mizjojo, Jimbob, Cruella and Dabidee were still not back from sector three yet.

Applejack, Ted and Jade arrived with Windooraa and Gorgon.

Twiggs and Bur checked in. "Sector one - negative."

Kroxy Jnr checked in. "Sector six – negative."

Rhyco checked in. "sector five - negative."

Pandoo shook his head and said "sorry, sector four - negative."

The only area on the control board that hadn't been scored off was sector three.

"What's in sector three?" asked Windooraa.

"The dungeon" said Gorgon.

"Give me strength! Why didn't we start there? Everyone, to the dungeon!" said Windooraa.

When they got to the dungeon, Twiggs and bur took them to the room that they last saw Sofo in.

It was damp, dark and smelly.

"yep, Cruella and Dabidee have definitely been in here" said Rhyco.

"Shh" said Windooraa.

Windooraa slowly walked around the room. Everyone was silent.

"I can feel It. Magic has been used in this room" she said.

Windooraa took out her crowbar wand and waved it.

A single spark shot out, and danced around the room, coming to a halt in the corner.

Windooraa waved her wand again and a magic portal opened in the corner.

"*Quick!* They went this way" said Windooraa as she stepped through the magic portal and disappeared from the room.

The others took a deep breath then followed her through.

Chapter 10. The red case.

Windooraa stepped through the portal first. She was now in a dark, cold forest. She waved her crowbar wand, and fireworks lit the sky above.

Everyone else was now through the portal.

"This is strange. This place looks dark and evil, but the light from your fireworks make it look like Bourbonville, just for a second" said Kroxalot.

"I think so too, but I assure you, we are not in Bourbonville. Everyone- gather round" Said Windooraa.

Windooraa shared her suspicions with the group.

"*Floof!*" yelled Kroxalot as Floof flew through the air, in a ninja like flying hug.

Sofo, mizJojo, Jimbob, Cruella and Dabidee were running towards them too, along with the forest people.

"We saw the fireworks. I knew it was you" said Sofo, relieved to see everyone.

They all hugged.

"Sofo, how did you get here?" asked Windooraa.

"A shadow-witch brought us here" said Sofo.

"Yeah, it was a shadow-witch that brought us here too. Wee Floaty purple thing, with a red case". Said Dabidee.

Windooraa smiled then said, "Take me to the first place you saw this Witch".

Chapter 11. The mirror of darkness.

Sofo and Floof took everyone back to the castle ruins.

Windooraa shot a firework above the castle ruin, and for a second it looked just like castle Rox.

When they all got to the dungeon room, it was different this time.

In the middle of the room stood a tall rectangular object, covered in cloth. "That wasn't here before" said Sofo.

Windooraa removed the cloth, and there stood a mirror.

"That's spooky" said Gorgon. "There's no reflection in it."

Windooraa waved her wand in the direction of the mirror.

The mirror turned darker for a second, and then slowly the Shadow-Witch began to appear in the mirror.

The shadow-Witch didn't move. "Be careful! The last time she sucked us into that red case" warned Sofo.

Windooraa smiled then said, "my sister had a red case like that". Then quick as a flash Windooraa threw her crowbar wand into the Mirror, smashing it to pieces.

Smoke filled the room.

When the smoke faded, there stood a beautiful girl, with lovely eyes, and long purple hair.

"Daniellah!" said Windooraa as she hugged her.

Everyone was silent.

"Hrrm, hrrm, who is Daniellah, and Can I hug her next?" asked Buttshot with a cheeky smile.

The girl turned to them all. "I am Daniellah, I am Windooraa's sister. I have been trapped here in Pumpkinville since long, long ago."

Cruella was confused and asked "Eh? how did you get trapped? You trapped us."

"A long, long time ago, when Bourbonville was just a new city, I was fighting a terrible evil, called Vijjilanti.

We couldn't stop Vijjilanti for good, so the only way we could save Bourbonville was to trap her.

I trapped her inside my magic case, but I was worried she would break out, so I took the case inside the mirror to make sure Bourbonville was safe.

I didn't realise it at the time, but by taking Vijjilanti into the mirror, I created a mirror version of Bourbonville, a dark and lonely place.

My magic alone was not strong enough to let me come back home, that's why I brought you here. I'm sorry I scared you all".

Daniellah looked to the forest people and said "I'm so sorry I brought you here with me.

I didn't realise you were in Bourbonville forest when I trapped Vijjilanti in my case. Thank you for fighting all the pumpkins and all the bears for so long. It is you alone that have stopped Vijjilanti from becoming too powerful.

I wish I could have gotten you home.

"Well, there's no time like the present" said Windooraa, and she swished her wand.

Dabidee and Cruella joined her and swished their wands too.

"Now Daniellah! We need your power too. Take us home!" said Windooraa.

Daniellah held up her red case, and blinked her eyes, and the portal opened.

"Let's go everyone. To Bourbonville!" Cheered Jimbob.

Chapter 12. The BBQ.

Back in Bourbonville, everyone was at the party in the castle gardens.

Handsome Dave set up the karaoke machine, which amazed Cherrypee, who was busy making a list of songs to sing to everyone.

Pandoo was at the BBQ singing to himself. ...

♪sizzle, sizzle, sizzle,

I love sizzle,

let's all sizzle,

Pork- Cho-oh-oh-ohps! ♫

Rhyco and Kroxy were really interested in the forest people, and they were already making plans to fly cloud cars with Flipflop and Buttshot.

Floof was so excited. Not just because everyone was back in Bourbonville, but because he could hear Pandoo sing his favourite song. The sizzle song. Floof ran around in circles, shaking his butt, and accidentally knocked over Daniella's red case.

Smoke started to ooze out of the red case. Its darkness covered everything that it touched.

An evil laugh echoed across the sky.

It was Vijjilanti.

Chapter 13. The battle for Bourbonville.

The sky filled with clouds and rain. Lightning flashed, and struck Castle Rox, setting fire to the tower.

Wind blew the windows in and sent cloud cars flying into each other.

Clouds started to form into a huge, dark floating head in the sky.

"At last! I am free! Nothing can stop my darkness!" Roared Vijjilanti.

From underneath Vijjilanti, an army of Pumpkins - ten thousand strong, marched towards the castle.

Everyone was in shock.

Daniellah shouted *"Everyone, run! Run! Get out of here. I will trap Vijjilanti again. Save yourselves!"*

"No" said Applejack "This is Bourbonville and we do things together here".

"Everyone! Get ready for battle" declared Kroxalot.

The forest people charged first. Running with their swords held high, straight for the pumpkins. They were warriors.

Pumpkin guts sprayed all over the fields.

Kroxy Jnr and Rhyco joined them, using their cloud cars to mow down rows of pumpkins.

Potts and Quackmore got on Roy the dragons back and flew above the pumpkins, torching them with Roy's fire.

Applejack, Ted and Jade were high in the sky, dropping boulders, smashing the pumpkins below.

Twiggs and Bur shot arrows at a pack of bears, that had just joined the pumpkins.

Pandoo was using a large pork chop as a bat to hit coals from the BBQ at the pumpkins, setting them on fire.

Handsome Dave was in full commando gear, ripping pumpkins in half.

A bear tried to get Penny, so Handsome Dave done a triple Lutz spinning kick, kicking the bear's head clean off- hurtling it into another bear, knocking it out.

Jimbob was using his glitter cannon to blind the bears.

Kroxalot, Gorgon and Mizjojo were slashing their way through the field with their swords.

Sofo and Floof were throwing science potions at the pumpkins, which exploded on impact.

They were winning.

Windooraa, Daniellah, Dabidee and Cruella had made their way to Vijjilanti.

Their wands were exploding full of colour and sparks as they took aim at Vijjilanti.

"Quick everyone! Join our magic!" yelled Dabidee.

They focused the magic beams from their wands, and Daniellah's case together, making a super magic beam, 10 times bigger.

"*Now!*" shouted Cruella, and they shot their beam straight at Vijjilanti.

At first Vijjilanti got smaller, but then her evil laugh filled the sky once more, and she became even bigger than before.

"You can't beat me this time! My darkness is too strong! "Die! roared Vijjilanti, as lightning shot across the battlefield.

Chapter 14. What a remarkable woman.

Sofo could not hear anything, apart for the ringing in her ears.

Her head hurt again, and she felt dizzy.

She fell to her knees, scared, looking for help, as fear crept into her heart.

They were losing.

A bear had broken Floof's paw.

The forest people had been overrun by pumpkins. There were too many pumpkins to fight. There was no way they could win. Potts and Quackmore were on the ground, helping Roy, after lightning had struck his tail.

Handsome Dave and Penny were trapped by pumpkins. Handsome Dave would have kept fighting but gave up after the pumpkins had tied Penny up in pumpkin vines.

Jimbob had ran out of glitter, and Pandoo's pork chop-bat had snapped.

Rhyco and Kroxy Jnr had flown so fast, and hard in their cloud cars, that they ran out of glitter, causing their clouds to fall out of the sky, into the fields below.

Applejack, Ted and Jade had crashed into each other in one of Vijjilanti's black clouds, knocking themselves to the ground.

Mizjojo, Gorgon and Kroxalot were still fighting, but they were tired now. Their swords were getting slower, and now there were even more bears headed straight for them.

Sofo looked across the field and saw Windooraa, Daniellah, Dabidee and Cruella on the ground. Unconscious.

Sofo began to cry.

She felt all hope, disappear from her heart.

She was so tired, weak and sore that She fell to the ground, and closed her eyes. Everything went dark.

A muffled thud on the ground beside her made her open her eyes. She could hardly see.

Then, slowly coming into focus, she could make out a pair of boots, covered in glitter.

"Don't give up Sofo" said a familiar voice.

"Get up!" said the voice, this time lifting her to her feet.

It was Jimbob.

Sofo hugged him.

"It's no use Jimbob, Vijjilanti is too powerful, we can't defeat her darkness" she cried.

Through her tears she could see Jimbob in front of her, holding something.

Jimbob said; "My old pal Pee-lee used to say, the best way to fight the dark, is with the light.

Sometimes, when I get scared, she leaves an angel feather for me on the ground, to remind me there is always someone with me, and no matter what, there is always hope.

Here, she would want you to have this one" and he handed Sofo a beautiful white feather.

Sofo looked at the feather. It was white and fluffy, but just a feather.

But then, she turned it on its side, and a flash of light made it glow brighter.

Sofo didn't feel cold anymore.

Her head didn't hurt, and she was starting to hear again.

Sofo stared at the feather, her heart was pounding.

The Hope that had disappeared moments ago, flooded back through her whole body, and She felt alive.

She heard Vijjilanti's laughter fill the sky again, But Sofo wasn't scared anymore.

"Thank you Jimbob" said Sofo as she turned to face Vijjilanti.

Sofo stood in the middle of the battlefield.

Vijjilanti was looking right at her, then took a deep breath, sucking in all the air around, then blew out a huge fireball straight at Sofo.

Sofo held up her hand to try and protect herself.

The feather in her hand shone bright, stopping the fireball, then pushed it safely away from Sofo.

"No!" screamed Vijjilanti.

Sofo stuck her feet fast to the ground. Holding the feather tight, she thrust her hand forward, pushing with all her might. She could feel magic rushing through her whole body.

Her feather glowed even brighter this time. Brighter than a star. It started to form a jet at the end of the feather.

Growing, getting bigger, and bigger and then shot out in a blast from the feather, straight through Vijjilanti's face.

Vijjilanti tried to scream but nothing came out. She exploded and turned to ash.

The pumpkin army became still. No longer able to move under Vijjilanti's spell.

The bears turned into really muscly mice and ran away.

As the ash started to clear, letting the sun back into the sky, everyone cheered.

Sofo walked over to Daniellah, who was, smiling but had tears in her eyes.

"Why are you crying? We are safe now" said Sofo.

"I was just thinking about how powerful she was" said Daniellah.

"Don't worry, she's gone now. We won" said Sofo.

Daniellah shook her head then said "No. Not Vijjilanti. I meant how powerful Pee-Lee was.

It was Pee-Lee that taught me my magic when I was little.

It was her that helped me make my red case, and it was her that helped me trap Vijjilanti a long, long time ago.

I'm not crying because I'm sad, I'm crying because I'm happy.

I just realised that it was also because of Pee-Lee's love and memories, that you were strong enough to beat Vijjilanti too.

What a remarkable woman."

Chapter 15. The Halloween Ball.

Sofo loved a party at castle Rox.

Everyone was singing again. Together in Bourbonville.

♪We're all going to a party tonight …

We're all going to a party tonight …

We're all going to a party tonighhhhhhhht ♪

Chapter 16. It's just the beginning.

Kroxy Jnr had not been in his janitor's hut for a while now, which made it a perfect place for a gang of really muscly mice to make a new home ...

To be Continued.

From Granny P's imagination workshop

Lightning Source UK Ltd.
Milton Keynes UK
UKHW050323280521
384514UK00002B/35